TOMBSTONES

Volume 3

The Rowan Tree

13 Digit ISBN 978-1532982248
10 Digit ISBN 1532982240

Printed in the United States of America

The characters and events in this book are fictitious. Any similarity to real persons, living, dead, or undead is coincidental and not intended by the author.

Living in constant fear and loss of sleep is intended by the author.

Tombstonesbooks.com 2016

PART ONE

DEVLIN

THE ROWAN TREE
Chapter 1
September 29, 1966

The sound of the steel blade striking the ground
was both comforting and ominous. The soil was soft
and heavy from the rain that came in a steady
downpour. The body lay in the burlap sack next to him
on the other side of the hole from where he piled the
dirt. The pile seemed to accumulate more slowly with
each shovel. The sack was small and lifeless, thank God.

The sky was black, only punctuated by the
occasional crack of lightening that lit up the landscape
with a flash. It illuminated the metal shovel, and every
time, it momentarily caused him to freeze for fear of

being seen by a late-night wanderer. The rain on the brown sack caused the outline of the motionless body to show through, revealing—to him at least—the horrible contents that he was trying to hide.

How deep would he need to dig to keep the body covered and safe from a stray dog? It was his son after all. He deserved some sort of proper burial, even though no one could ever visit or even know the location of the grave.

Shovel after shovel, the pile got taller and the hole got deeper. Time was not on his side. Dawn would appear sooner than he thought, and he could not be seen out here. His face was drenched with the rain, sweat, tears, and the blood of his young son.

Finally, with as much tenderness as fear, he picked up his son, careful to leave him in the burlap sack, and fell to his knees in the mud. He held him for a moment, thinking that any second the lifeless body might jerk back to life with one final attack. But the body was still. He lowered it into the muddy hole as a bolt of lightning struck nearby, scaring him back to reality and the understanding that he must finish his job quickly.

He took out the gold necklace from his pocket and held it in the palm of his hand. Water pooled around it and dripped down the length of the chain. He closed his fingers tightly around it and closed his eyes, silently hoping that this would somehow absolve him.

Then he got down on his knees and carefully placed it on top of the burlap sack.

Did that move? No, just the rain coming down.

He rose and began furiously shoveling the pyramid of dirt back into the secret grave. Within minutes, it was just a patch of dirt once again. Just a patch of dirt...with something evil percolating underneath.

THE ROWAN TREE
Chapter 2
Two Days Before—7:30 a.m.

      Tanner walked into the den and found his brother, Devlin, sitting amongst a collection of toys randomly strewn about the room. While Tanner was eight, seven years older than his baby brother, he felt uncomfortable being alone in the same room with him. He felt ashamed of this feeling. After all, Devlin was just a little toddler.

      He tried to explain his feelings...that his brother was just so young and delicate...that his uneasiness of being alone with him was just because babies could get hurt easily and he didn't want to be responsible. Or maybe, even as an eight-year-old, he could rationalize his feelings as perhaps a bit of jealousy or annoyance at having to put up with the nuisances that come along with having a younger sibling.

But he knew it was neither of these. Somehow, Tanner knew that Devlin just didn't seem to like him. He knew that he was not welcome in the room. He got that sense even when his parents were there too, not from them, but from the look in his brother's eyes. The sideways glances, the sometimes outright stares that forced Tanner to have to look away.

This time, Devlin didn't seem to notice that he had entered the room. Tanner halted a few steps in as his brother sat in the middle of the room, playing with a set of wooden alphabet blocks. He was stacking them in a tower, five or six high.

The tower tumbled, and Devin's brow furrowed in anger. He didn't scream or cry. He simply stared at the pile of randomly scattered letters. He stared, forehead wrinkled, for a full minute, seemingly oblivious to the fact that Tanner was standing just inside the entryway, observing him.

Slowly, he reached for one block and turned it in his hands. He carefully set it in place. His eyes searched for another. He reached out, turned it over, and set it down exactly next to the first. Again, he scanned the pile until he chose the third and so forth.

D-E-V-L-I-N

He had spelled his name! He was just one year old. He could barely speak...just a few simple words...yet he spelled his name? Tanner stood there, amazed by what he was watching. He wanted to call out for his mother to come and see but didn't want Devlin to know he was there. He remained motionless.

Devlin reached over slowly and picked up the N and held it in his right hand. With his left, he picked up the L and set it back down where the N had been.

D-E-V-I-L

At first, Tanner didn't get it. It was just a different grouping of letters. But the moment his mind recognized what he was looking at, he shifted his gaze from the blocks to his brother.

Devlin slowly raised his head, and his eyes fixed on Tanner. His eyes penetrated Tanner, almost commanding him not to move. A grin started to form on Devlin's face, but his eyes never changed. Tanner tried to yell out, but he was frozen in place.

Without looking down, the baby took his left hand and removed the letter L and set it aside. Then he picked up the V and held it in his right hand. He then picked up the I and placed it between the D and the E.

D-I-E

Tanner's mouth opened in a silent scream, still unable to get his body to move...unable to utter a sound.

Devlin looked down at the V in his hand. He turned it around, felling the weight of it. He tossed it in the air a few inches and caught it again in his tiny hand.

Then he looked back at Tanner, and his grin turned into a frown.

He cocked his arm backwards and threw the block straight at Tanner's face. Tanner saw it coming but was helpless to move and was unable to dodge it. The point of the block hit him square in the forehead, puncturing the skin and waking Tanner from his trance.

Immediately, Devlin began to cry, screaming hysterically as only babies can do, as if he were somehow the one harmed. Tanner ran out of the room.

Devlin unscrambled the letters on the floor in front of him and resumed playing as if nothing had happened.

THE ROWAN TREE
Chapter 3
7:45 a.m.

Running frantically from the room, holding his head, Tanner screamed, "Mom! Help! Where are you?"

His mother, having already heard the screams of the baby, was running from the kitchen and down the hallway. "What's wrong? What's happened?" she yelled.

She was instinctively running to the sound of her crying baby, but Tanner ran right to her, nearly tackling her, and jumped into her arms. She lifted him up and saw the fear in Tanner's face...the blood running down his forehead.

"Oh, Tanner, honey…my word! What happened?" she asked as she pulled him closer to her as she continued running down the hall to check on Devlin, whose cry had alerted her in the first place.

"Devlin was playing with the blocks and he was spelling out—" he blurted out frantically and then realized how crazy he would seem. "Well, he picked up a block and threw it at me and hit me in the head," he said, holding on to his mother.

Still holding him, she reached the entrance to the room where Devlin was playing, moving quickly to check on her other son.

As she turned the corner, Tanner began screaming, "No, Ma! Don't take me back in there!" He tightened his grip around her and buried his face into her shoulder, begging not to go back in the room with Devlin.

"Honey? What on earth is wrong?" she asked, wiping his tears and looking more closely at the small wound on his forehead. But Tanner kept his face stubbornly against his mother's shoulder so that Devlin could not see him.

"TAKE ME OUT OF HERE!" he wailed, his voice muffled by his tears and her shirt.

His mother looked up to check on Devlin, but he was calmly playing with a toy fire truck, crawling on his knees and guiding it through a maze of blocks on the floor. He didn't even bother to look up to acknowledge their presence in the room.

"Devlin? Honey? Is everything okay?" she asked.

The baby just kept guiding his fire truck, occasionally stopping to place a firefighter on board or to take one off.

She watched him curiously for another five or ten seconds until finally leaving and taking Tanner to the living room. She sat with him in the rocking chair and soothingly stroked his hair and spoke softly to him in his ear.

Tanner did not want to leave his mother's side. He felt much safer not being alone in the house. And when his dad came home, he knew everything would be all right.

Devlin continued playing with his fire truck. He was not happy knowing that his mother was holding Tanner in her arms. He always hated that. He pushed harder and harder on the plastic truck, running it back and forth on the carpet, until finally the wheel snapped off. Slowly, his face turned from anger into a wide, satisfied grin.

THE ROWAN TREE
Chapter 4
Lunchtime

"Taaanner!" his mother called at the base of the steps. "Lunch is ready....Come on down!"

"Can you bring it up to my room?" Tanner yelled back. "I'm doing something. Can I just eat up here?"

"Take a break for a few minutes," she replied. "We don't eat in the bedroom, and you know that."

"I'm not hungry," he tried meekly.

"And I don't care," his mother said jokingly. "It's lunchtime, and that's all there is to it."

Tanner had been in his bedroom for the past three hours with his door shut. He did not want to be anywhere near Devlin. Because his mother kept the stairs blocked with a baby gate so Devlin wouldn't climb them, he was able to relax a bit if he stayed on a different floor altogether.

Nervously, he cracked his bedroom door and peeked up and down the hallway. Nothing. He cautiously stepped out and tiptoed in socks down the old wooden steps. Every creak betrayed him. He walked wide-legged so that he didn't step right in the middle of each stair to reduce the noise. He knew he looked like a moron, but he didn't care.

Once at the bottom, he hurdled the kid fence and sprinted into the kitchen to the safety of his mother. Devlin was seated in his high chair at the table, and Tanner did not look him straight in the eyes. He went to the table, picked up the plate with his peanut butter and jelly sandwich on it and his glass of milk, and sat at the complete opposite end.

Devlin stared at him the entire time.

His mother sat down next to Devlin and began to feed him. Devlin ate, all the while never taking his gaze off of Tanner, who sat with his head down, eating quickly.

His mother finally noticed that Tanner was sitting at the opposite end from his normal chair. She turned to him and said, "Honey, why are you sitting all the way over there?"

Upon hearing his brother being called "honey", the baby spit out some of the food that he was chewing onto the tray of the high chair.

Tanner didn't answer.

"Seriously, sweetie, won't you come join us over here?" she asked.

This time, Devlin spit the food out onto the side of his mother's face and pounded his tiny fist on the high chair.

His mother turned immediately to the angry baby and said, "Devlin! What is wrong with you?" as she wiped the mushed carrots off of her cheek.

Devlin just stared angrily at her.

"That is not the way we act at the table!" she scolded. "Look at your brother. See how nicely he is eating?"

With that, the baby took his gaze from his mother and shifted it over to Tanner. Tanner looked up sheepishly for one brief moment, caught Devlin's stare, and looked back down at his plate. Devlin jerked his head back towards his mother, and this time, instead of spitting a little, he opened up his mouth in a huge, cavernous gape. Then, like a fire hose, he released a stream of disgusting orange bile all over his mother's face, drenching her clothing and her hair and knocking her out of her seat.

She scrambled to her feet, frantically wiping the chunky stench from her eyes and mouth. Tanner stared open-mouthed at the scene unfolding before him. His mother went to the sink and splashed water all over her face, trying to keep from throwing up herself.

Breathing hard, she turned back to the baby in the high chair to try to understand what had just happened. Tanner, now crying, had backed away from the table and was standing with his back against the far wall.

Her maternal instincts returned to her once again. She rushed over to the high chair to get Devlin and make sure he was okay.

Tanner yelled out, "Mom! NO!"

But his mother went to pick up the baby. As she reached out, Devlin flashed an evil glance at Tanner as if to warn him to stay away. And then suddenly, Devlin snatched the fork that was on the high chair tray and plunged it into the back of his mother's hand.

Tanner rushed over and grabbed his mother away from the high chair while she screamed in agony. She staggered over to the sink and pulled the fork out. Blood was running down her arm, and a trail of drops lay on the floor.

She ran the wound under the cold water and then wrapped a dish towel around it to stop the bleeding. The pain was bearable. She was more concerned about Tanner, who was crying with his arms wrapped tightly around her.

"Okay, honey, I'm all right," she said, consoling Tanner.

She looked back at the high chair to try to understand what had just happened.

It was empty.

THE ROWAN TREE
Chapter 5

The baby was gone.

He had been in the high chair. And he had been completely strapped in. He had never gotten out of the chair by himself before.

The kitchen looked like a crime scene. Drops of blood led from the sink to the table. Orange bile covered part of the high chair and most of the table itself. The chair that she had been sitting on was knocked over, and more puke dripped from the table onto it. Tanner's chair was also upended. And on the high chair lay the fork with blood on the tongs.

She and Tanner both scanned the kitchen floor for the baby, but he was nowhere to be seen.

"Devlin?" she called. "Devlin...where are you?"

She slowly walked over to the high chair, and there she saw two footprints in a puddle of the rancid throw up. From there, she could see the orange trail of tiny feet leading out of the kitchen and down the hallway.

She tentatively followed the prints. Tanner followed her but stayed a safe distance behind. He certainly did not want to be left in the kitchen alone.

"Devlin? Honey? Are you okay?" she called with both concern and fear.

The house was silent. She had forgotten about the pain in her hand, although she was clutching it. She was much more concerned with finding her baby. But she also had this embarrassing fear of her own one-year-old. What kind of mother was afraid of her own baby? She tried to act as calmly as possible, both for her own sanity and to keep Tanner from freaking out.

The footprints led back into the playroom. There was only one way in and one way out of this room. He would have to be in here.

And as she turned the corner, there he sat amongst the blocks with his favorite toy, his now broken fire truck, rolling it back and forth over and over again.

THE ROWAN TREE
Chapter 6
5:30 p.m.

She didn't know what she should say to him when he got home from work. After all, he was her husband and the boy's father, but did things *really* happen the way she remembered them? A few hours removed from the events at lunchtime, everything had calmed down.

Sure, Tanner had a mark on his forehead, but that kind of thing happens to kids. Did Devlin actually throw the block? If he did, it must have been accidental. And now in retrospect, of course, Devlin had gotten sick or choked on his food. Sure, the sheer volume and force of the projectile vomiting was shocking to say the least, but he was just a baby, and babies do that from time to time.

And she could even explain away the bandage on her hand to herself. She thought Devlin was old enough to start using a fork. So what had happened was he was choking on his vomit and became frantic. His arms started flailing and, in the process, the fork ended up in the back of her hand. Of course, there were explanations. She would have been crazy to think otherwise.

Right?

"But those eyes…" she thought to herself.

She felt ashamed that the first emotion that crossed her mind when she looked at him was fear. Again, she wondered what kind of mother would be afraid of her own baby. She had to force it out of her mind and intentionally go and pick him up, thinking about whether to change his diaper or to just sit with him in her lap. Luckily, Tanner wasn't around to witness her hesitation since he had basically barricaded himself in his room for the afternoon.

So, by the time Devlin's father came home from work, all he was told was that Devlin had been extremely sick and she had had a horrible afternoon hosing down the kitchen, airing out the stench from the vomit, and rebandaging the wound on her hand.

When Tanner heard his mother talking to his father downstairs, he shot out of his bedroom door and ran down the creaky wooden steps, this time oblivious to the noise he was making.

"Dad! Dad!" he screamed, with eyes as wide as saucers. "I don't want to stay here...keep Devlin away from me!"

"Whoa, cowpoke," his father said, picking him up. Tears were running down Tanner's face, and he looked absolutely terrified. "Hey, hey, calm down...what's the matter?"

Tanner looked down at his hands. He didn't want to say it too loud. He knew if Devlin heard it he would be angry again.

In a soft, somewhat muffled voice, he said, "Devlin said he doesn't want me here, and if I talk to Mom he's going to kill me."

THE ROWAN TREE
Chapter 7
Midnight

      Tanner could not sleep. The shadows on the wall were a comforting distraction from his imagination, but they could not keep his fear at bay. In his mind, the baby was small enough to be anywhere. Of course he would be under the bed. And Tanner knew that if he rolled onto his side, when he rolled back, the baby would be on the other side of the pillow, waiting to attack.

      He had asked his father to keep his door open and the hall light on. But seeing Devlin's room across the hall with his door cracked made it even worse. He jumped out of bed, careful to land a far enough distance away so that the baby couldn't grab his ankles from under the bed when his feet hit the floor. Then he darted across the room, shut the door all the way, and leaped back into bed.

Devlin could not sleep either. His anger consumed him. His door was cracked open as it usually was, and that was good. Reaching the doorknob would not have gone unheard since he would have had to slide over a box and stand on it.

He heard Tanner shut his door and leap back into bed. That changed his plans. With an open door, the boy would have been so easy. But now, instead of dealing with Tanner, he'd have his mother come to him. He pulled up the mattress in his crib and made sure the kitchen knife he had taken earlier in the day was in a spot where he could reach it quickly.

She heard the baby cry. She actually felt some relief that it was a normal baby thing to do. Lying in bed, her mind had been racing with concern over the weird behavior that Devlin was exhibiting. She wanted desperately to believe that he was just a normal baby— that maybe he was just different in a good way, not a freak.

She got up quickly so as not to wake her husband and shuffled down the hallway. As she pushed open the door, the moonlight illuminated the room enough that she could see Devlin sitting in the crib, crying for her with his arms outstretched.

"Awww, poor baby," she said in a low voice as she picked up her crying child. "What's wrong? Did the moonlight wake you up?"

And then, in her ear, softly at first, the baby said his first words, but the voice was not that of a baby, or even a child. In a deep, husky whisper, he said, "I've been up all night….WAITING FOR YOU!"

And with that, the two pudgy hands grabbed her neck, and he squeezed as hard as he could. Her eyes opened wide and she tried to scream, but the grip was too tight. She spun around the room with the baby not lessening his grip, struggling to take a breath. Her hand clutched at his arms frantically and, finally, was able to rip free from the deadly grasp.

She ran to the crib and hurled the baby into it, horrified by the creature that still looked exactly like the child she loved so much. Devlin lifted up the mattress and removed the knife from its hiding place, placed it between his teeth, and began scaling the rungs of the crib.

She stumbled backwards towards the door, screaming for help. Once in the hallway, she turned to run down to the bedroom but slipped on the rug. From around the corner came the baby, the large knife blade in his mouth, crawling quickly towards her. She crab-walked backwards, trying desperately to make it to her bedroom door, but the baby was gaining on her.

Devlin caught up to her and climbed over her flailing legs until his entire body was resting on her stomach. He put his left hand on her jaw and, with his other hand, took the knife out of his mouth. He raised it over his head. A voice emerged from deep down inside of him. It was a deep voice of a creature, not a baby, and he was speaking some sort of unrecognizable language.

His father opened the door and lunged at the two of them, diving onto his wife's body to take the blow of the plunging knife. The blade dug partially into his shoulder but stopped at the bone. The force of his dive knocked the baby off of her and sent him tumbling down the steep wooden stairs.

There were no sounds except for the heavy breathing and tears from his mother. With a rush of adrenalin, the father ignored the knife that was protruding from his back. All he felt was the warm trickle of blood falling down his spine. He stood, looked down at his wife, and then reached over his shoulder and yanked hard at the blade in his back. The pain finally arrived as he wiggled the knife free.

What the heck just happened? he thought. *That was Devlin, right?*

He peered over the edge of the stairs. At the bottom of the stairwell, his baby lay in a heap, motionless. His neck was twisted at an impossible angle, as was his right arm. His son was dead.

THE ROWAN TREE
Chapter 8
12:30 a.m.

Their child was dead. Tanner's brother was dead. But they had all seen that it really wasn't a normal baby. Maybe it had been some sort of weird affliction, some syndrome. Probably not, especially with him speaking an archaic language. They all knew for certain that it was something supernatural, a demon, something unexplainable.

They had loved Devlin. But this was not Devlin.

They wanted to call the police and tell them what had happened. But how could they? No one would believe that a baby was terrorizing them and that this had been self-defense. It was even more innocent than that...it was an accident. He had not in any way tried to hurt the baby. He had just saved his wife's life by offering his own. The baby being knocked off was necessary. The fact that it occurred at the top of the stairs was just bad luck.

Or was it a stroke of good luck? The baby—or the thing, whatever it was—probably wouldn't have stopped simply because its parents scolded him. This evil being could have killed all of them.

But no matter how justified or accidental the circumstances, their child was dead. No explanation would have convinced the police that the father was not responsible, and he would therefore be punished. And it wouldn't have been just a light punishment; he would've been sentenced to prison, probably for the rest of his life.

They decided to lie. They would tell the police that the baby was missing and that it must have been taken during the night. They were already being punished by having their child taken from them by some maleficent force; they didn't want Tanner to suffer another blow by losing his father. There was no good solution.

He decided to bury it. But first he would get the necklace that had been given to Devlin by his grandmother at his birth. It was a gold Saint Benedict medallion. She had said it was meant to protect the wearer from harm. Well, that was a little late now. He hadn't believed that kind of thing, but with what he had just witnessed, he was willing to believe anything. There had to be some sort of ritual or remembrance. This had been his child. Well, at one point, it used to be his child.

And so he went to the basement, got a shovel and a burlap sack, and headed outside into the dark, rainy night. He trudged through the storm, wanting to put some distance between the burial site and the home. But he also wanted it to be where no one else would find it. He walked up the hill to the edge of his property.

With his face soaking wet with a mix of tears and rain, he selected the spot where he would bury his son.

THE ROWAN TREE
Chapter 9
Sunrise—6:46 a.m.

There had been no sleep. His guilt and confusion were too great. The loss of a child is traumatic for anyone. But what he and his family had been through would keep them awake at night for years to come.

He had stared out of the window and watched the storm all night. The grave was in sight, not too far from the house. He felt it should be close enough and on his own property so that it wouldn't be accidentally discovered.

As the sun rose and peeked over the tree line, his heart nearly stopped when he saw the grave in the light of day. Of course he would have to keep it unmarked and its location a secret. But what he saw now made it so obvious that his secret would certainly be exposed.

In the morning sunlight, the fresh earth covering the grave was completely visible. It would take months for grass to cover up the newly disturbed dirt. He would have to hide it better. In his mind, he was in a terrible rush. He had not called the police yet, but certainly a neighbor out on a morning stroll could stumble across it. And if they were questioned by the police, who knows if they would connect the dots?

Then the idea occurred to him. He would plant a tree in the same spot! Of course the ground would be dug up if he were planting a tree. And he would even put down mulch around the base. The grave would be totally concealed.

No one would ever know what was buried underneath.

INTERLUDE

THE ROWAN TREE
Chapter 10

Life did not get easier. Over the weeks and months that followed, the family would not be allowed to forget what had happened. Besides the police investigation, the thing that had once been Devlin would not let them move on.

It seemed that whenever there was another rainy night, the grave was disturbed. Just as the rowan tree was nourished by the rains, the grave itself seemed to be affected.

They would hear their names called out in the middle of the night. On nights when there were especially strong storms, they would occasionally even see things outside near the grave.

And worse, as time passed, voices from the grave could be heard inside the house. And when they started seeing spirits, it was decided that it was time for the family to move out. It would be another forty years until someone occupied the house once again.

PART TWO

THE INHABITANTS

THE ROWAN TREE
Chapter 11
June 6, 2006—10:14 a.m.

"Jeez, that took forever," said Max to no one in particular.

Max was thirteen, and his sister, Daisy, was eight. They had been in the car for the last four hours with their parents and their dog, Sam. They were moving to an old house in West Virginia after their father had decided that he could work from home since all he needed to manage his business was a phone line and an Internet connection.

Max's father, Phil, had inherited this piece of property and the house that stood on it nearly ten years ago from his Great Aunt Elizabeth. He had barely known her, but when she passed, he was the only living relative to be found. While he had been happily surprised to receive an unexpected gift of that magnitude, it turned out to be quite a challenge to realize any benefits from it.

Max's parents had put the property on the market almost immediately after the ink had dried on the inheritance paperwork at what was considered a fair price. It sat there for months with not even a single prospective buyer walking through. They lowered the price time and time again, but no one showed any interest in the property.

So when the economy slowed and Phil's clients became less frequent, they decided it was time to cut expenses. And the biggest expense was the mortgage. So they sold the townhouse on M Street in Georgetown and decided to move in to the old house in West Virginia, which for some reason no one wanted to buy.

Sam jumped out of the car and immediately started sniffing around for places to pee.

"Well, here we are, guys," said Phil. "Our own little piece of heaven right here on Short Mountain."

"It looks great," said Max. "This place looks awesome! C'mon, Daisy, I'll race you to the front door!"

"Hold on a second there!" yelled Phil. "Don't go up there empty-handed. Grab something from the trunk; we have a lot of stuff to move in."

While Phil loaded up each of the kids with a box to carry, Sam continued his search of the property by running around sniffing everything, stopping occasionally to urinate on whatever object he felt he should claim as his own.

When he made it to the side of the house about fifty yards away, he suddenly stopped in his tracks. He crouched lower and stared at the tree that stood all alone in the field. With a low, guttural growl, he walked towards it slowly, continuing to growl at the lonesome tree. Nothing else in the yard could grab his attention now.

Slowly, he moved forward, until finally he was at the base of the trunk. He began sniffing around the trunk of the tree, making a complete circle. He barked a few times, looking back to see if anyone was paying any attention to him, but they had all moved inside the house. He turned sideways and lifted his leg to mark his scent on this object too when, all of a sudden, a gust of wind stirred from out of nowhere and the lowest-hanging branch of the tree smacked him on the tail end with a *crack*!

Sam yelped and, with his tail between his legs, scampered off, whimpering with his head down towards the house.

It would be the last time he wandered anywhere near the tree.

THE ROWAN TREE
Chapter 12
10:15 p.m.

Max liked the new house and was thrilled to finally have a room of his own that he didn't have to share with his little sister. Not only was his room bigger than his old one, but he could also decorate it anyway he liked. No more princess posters on Daisy's side of the room. The entire room was going to be a temple to all things related to sports.

One difference he noticed from his old city life was that when the lights were out, it was deafly quiet. There was no evening traffic, no occasional police sirens, just the lazy sounds of crickets chirping. And while he thought it would be darker at night, it was actually fairly bright because the sky was so clear and the moonlight bled into his room.

Between the excitement of his new surroundings and the extreme silence, Max found himself lying in bed, staring at the ceiling, unable to drift off.

Maaaaaaax...

He heard what must have been the wind gently blowing outside his window. His brow furrowed a bit, but he chalked it up to sounds you hear in the country.

His mind went back to his new room. He had already put a few things up on the walls. The first thing he had hung right on the back of the door was his favorite poster—the cover of his favorite horror book, Ant Farm. It was a giant tombstone with a ghostly face on it with deadly red-eyed ants crawling over it. And it was actually signed by the author, Screamin Calhoun. He had not been allowed to hang it in his previous room because Daisy was afraid of it.

Maaaaaaaaaaaax...

That time he really thought he heard it.

He climbed out of bed, went to the window, and pulled the curtain aside.

Am I really hearing someone call my name?

Everything was still. The tall grass at the edge of the yard was blowing ever so slightly, but that was the only movement. But what caught his attention off in the distance was the tree. There were plenty of other trees around, but this specific one seemed to stand all alone, almost an outcast from the rest of the trees in the woods surrounding the house.

This tree was in the field off in the distance. Only the silhouette was visible, but he couldn't stop staring at it.

Maaaaaaaaaaax…

There was no way that was the wind. The windows were closed, and nothing moved in the yard. It actually seemed to be coming from inside his head.

But the tree… he thought. *It came from over by the tree…but even if there were somebody by the tree calling my name, it would be too far away for me to hear. The tree is fifty yards across the field.*

Suddenly, there was some slight movement. He squinted and tried to see the tree with greater detail. Under one of the branches, something was there. It might have been a person, but it seemed like a mist or fog. But it had some sort of form. It was a bluish grey light that undulated like a wave on the ocean. And the longer he watched it, the more lifelike it became.

Maaaaaaaaaaaax, it called.

This time he was sure of it, and it brought a smile to his face. He felt strangely at peace. Within minutes, he was blissfully asleep in his new room, happy with his new surroundings.

THE ROWAN TREE
Chapter 13
June 7th—The Following Morning

     The next morning, Max was up with the sunrise.
The moment he opened his eyes, he was out of bed,
getting dressed, and walking through the kitchen to the
front door.

     "Well, good morning, sunshine! Why are you up
so early?" asked his mother, who was sitting at the
kitchen table with a cup of coffee and the newspaper.

     The words kind of startled Max from his
sleepwalking, although he was wide awake.

     "Um...oh, yeah...hey...good morning," he
answered with a confused tone in his voice.

"Are you ready for some breakfast?" she asked. "I can make some eggs or even some pancakes if you'd like."

"Um, maybe later," he said, walking to the front door. "I'll be back in a little bit."

"What do you mean you'll 'be back in a little bit'?" she asked, laughing. "Where do you think you are going?"

And that's when the thought occurred to him. He really didn't know where he was going. He was just going, as if he had no control. He didn't even remember getting dressed.

"Oh...I was just...I was just gonna look around outside and explore a little," he stammered.

"Well, you certainly are up and at 'em," she said. "Are you sure you don't want something to eat first?"

"No, thanks, I'm not hungry yet."

"All right, well stay close," his mother answered. "You don't know your way around here just yet. Don't want to have to send out the search and rescue team for you."

Max headed out the front door and took a brief look around at his surroundings.

Maaaaaaaaaaaax...

Now he remembered why he was outside. He started in the direction of the open field with the tree standing in solitude. In the daylight, it seemed a little closer than he remembered from his window the previous night.

As he got closer, everything else around him seemed to disappear. He had no vision of anything like clouds, the woods, or the grass he was walking on. And everything was silent. Only a heartbeat, a continuous *thump thump, thump thump* rang in his ears. And the closer he got, the louder the heartbeat became.

Up close, the tree was magnificent. The roots stretched many yards beyond the tree and rose above and below the earth. In some places, the roots were completely out of the ground, creating tunnels large enough for Max's entire hand to fit under.

But the trunk was the most interesting. It had deep grooves and recesses, and in the middle, a large hollow area had formed, deep and dark enough that Max could not see completely to the bottom.

Max put his hand on the rough bark. To his surprise, the tree was warm to the touch. It felt good to have his hands on it.

THE ROWAN TREE
Chapter 14

The tree was covered with beautiful red berries. The colors were vibrant against the backdrop of the green leaves. Max picked one of the berries and put it in his mouth. He bit down, hoping it was not poisonous.

It wasn't sweet, but it wasn't really sour either. He decided he would pick a bunch and bring them to his mother. She was a terrific baker, and he was sure she would be able to make some sort of pie or something.

He rushed back to the house and returned with a bucket he was able to find in the shed outside of the house. Over the next hour, he picked berries from the low-hanging branches. When they were gone, he climbed up the trunk and went out on the limbs, picking until the bucket was nearly full.

A while later, he proudly walked into the kitchen and presented his mother with his gift towards the family dessert that night.

"Look, Mom!" he exclaimed with a huge smile on his face. "I collected all of these berries for you. Can you make them into something?"

"Oh, my word!" she said. "How long did it take you to pick all of these?"

"I don't know," he said. "Can you make something? Maybe a pie? Can I help?"

"Oh, honey, I don't know," she said with a bit of worry on her face. "I'm not even sure what kind of berries these are. I don't know if they are even edible."

"They are!" Max blurted out. "I ate one!"

"YOU DID WHAT?" she screamed in fear.

Within seconds, his mother was online researching the berries and the kind of tree to see if she had to rush her son to the emergency room.

After a few minutes, she had found the answer.

"Okay, Max," she said, shaking her head. "Well, you're lucky. These berries are from something called a rowan tree. Apparently you can eat them, but they are supposed to be cooked first. You might end up with a stomach ache, but you'll live. But in the future, don't just go around picking things off of bushes or the ground or whatever and putting them in your mouth. You are not a bear."

"Okay," Max said sheepishly. "But can we make them into a pie?"

"I already got a recipe online when I was trying to figure out if I had to start planning your funeral," she said with a smile.

She brought the bucket of berries over to the sink and told Max to pull up a kitchen chair. Together, they started washing the berries by placing them in a colander.

"There was some really interesting information online about that tree," said his mother. "Apparently, the rowan tree is a special tree that is native to England. In the old days, it was believed to offer protection against evil spirits. People were warned against removing or damaging the trees because their family would be cursed if they did."

"Cool!" grinned Max.

"But there were different viewpoints on whether the trees protected from evil or actually caused the evil. There was a woman in Scotland in the 1600s that was burned at the stake because they thought she was a witch when they found a rowan charm in her pocket. It was a twig from the tree tied with a red bow on it. There also is a legend that the tree is where the devil hanged his wife," she said, making a mockingly scary face.

"That's the coolest tree ever!" shouted Max. "We have a haunted tree!"

Laughing, she reached into the bucket for another handful of berries to wash.

"OWWW!" she screamed.

Max looked down, and on his mother's hand was a giant furry tarantula crawling up her arm! She shook her arm frantically, and the spider went flying into the sink. It landed in the colander of berries and then scurried out and went down the drain.

Max flipped on the switch to start the garbage disposal, and the motor roared to life. A disgusting sound of crushing bones and mangled fur made them wince in horror. Blood gurgled up through the drain like a witch's cauldron. Some blood was dripping from his mother's wrist. She turned on the faucet and held her hand under the cold water while she watched her blood mix with the tarantula's and float, with the rest of its body, down the drain.

THE ROWAN TREE
CHAPTER 15

Over the next few days, Max spent every day around the tree. From sunrise to sunset, he played under or around the tree. And every night, he looked out of his window, across the field at the tree, wishing it were morning again.

The heartbeat was ever-present. Max was used to it by now, and it was actually comforting to him. When he lay in his bed, he also heard the sound of leaves rustling and wood creaking. It was very faint, but Max knew where it was coming from. And every morning when he walked out the door to return to his hangout, it seemed the tree was a bit closer than it had been the day before.

54

THE ROWAN TREE
Chapter 16
The Third Day

Max was out the door like a bolt of lightning heading toward the tree. The screen door slammed behind him.

"Hey, speed racer!" his father called from in front of the wooden shed. "Come over here and look at my project for the day."

Max begrudgingly stopped and walked over to the shed. He really wanted to be up at the tree. It felt like he hadn't eaten in a week and the tree was his food. He needed it.

His father stood by the door holding a long, thick rope, and at his feet lay a huge, dirty old tire.

"Uh...this is your project for the day?" joked Max. "It looks like you are missing three other tires, and the rest of the car!"

"Very funny," said his father, laughing. "No, I'm making a tire swing! I figured since you were spending half your summer up by that tree, you and Daisy should have something fun to do there."

"Me and Daisy?" Max said, concerned.

His mind immediately forgot about the tire swing and focused on his little sister. He didn't mind hanging out with her, but for some reason, he felt that the tree was not a place for her.

"Aw, I don't think she would want to be up there with that old tree," he said, kicking the dirt with his sneaker.

"Oh, yes I would!" said Daisy, bouncing out from inside of the shed. "This is gonna be the best tire swing ever!"

His father picked up the tire and threw the rope over his shoulder.

"Come on, guys, let's get started."

Together, the three of them hiked across the field and up the hill to the tree. Max's normal level of excitement was replaced with a sense of dread. He didn't know why, but he felt very uncomfortable around the tree with his sister and father there.

The tree seemed different. The bark seemed darker. The roots seemed gnarlier, like angry snakes. The leaves seemed to pull back like cats' ears when they are angry and ready to attack. Max was aware of the heartbeat in his head, not his, but the heartbeat of the tree. It was faster than normal, and it made him nervous.

His father tied one end of the rope around the tire and threw the other end up and over the largest branch available. In a few minutes, he had it tied tightly, and the swing was ready for business.

"Oooo, let me go first, let me go first!" squealed Daisy.

"Hold on there," said her father. "Let me make sure this is safe."

He put both of his feet on the tire and stood on it while holding on to the rope. He bounced up and down, putting all of his weight on it.

"Well, if it can hold my big butt, it's cleared for you all," he said, laughing.

Daisy got on, and her father gave her a nice big push. Max grew more and more uncomfortable with each farther reach Daisy made into the sky. He didn't know how to explain it. The tree was his friend. *Friend?* He wasn't jealous; he just had a feeling that the tree didn't like being bothered like this. The rope around the tree seemed like a leash on a cat. It naturally resisted it and felt angry.

"Well, okay, you two," said Max's father. "Have fun, but be safe. Only one of you on the swing at a time."

And with that, he headed back down to the house, leaving Max and Daisy with the tree.

Daisy glided back and forth effortlessly, enjoying the wind through her hair.

The heartbeat got louder...and faster.

Stop it! Let her be. She's just a little girl!

"Daisy...um...c'mon, get off the swing now," Max pleaded with her. "Let's go and play something else."

She doesn't mean any harm! Please leave her alone!

"Come on, Daisy!" Max begged. "Get off the swing, I mean it!"

"Okay, okay," Daisy conceded. "I'm getting off."

But just as she finished her sentence, the tree limb started to creak loudly.

Max looked up and this time yelled out loud to the tree, "DON'T DO IT!"

The limb snapped with a huge *crack*! Daisy was at the top of her swing when, suddenly, the branch gave way, and she went hurtling from the sky onto the ground below. She landed with a thud, and the thick tree limb fell directly onto her arm, pinning her under it.

Max rushed over to her and, with all of his strength, lifted the branch just enough for Daisy to remove her arm. She rolled out from underneath, crying hysterically. The arm hung in a way that it was not supposed to, and Max knew immediately that it was broken and he needed his father.

Max ran to the house, tears streaming down his face, to get his father.

It's not funny! Why are you laughing? She's just a little girl! Okay...I know I shouldn't have brought her up here...I promise it won't happen again...

Max knew what had happened. He didn't understand how he knew, but he just knew.

THE ROWAN TREE
Chapter 17

The tree was closer. Max knew it. He expected it to be closer because he could hear it moving in the middle of the night. He could hear the heartbeat in his head. That was constant. But during the nights, he could hear the roots ripping from the ground and burying themselves just a bit closer.

He opened his eyes as he lay in bed. His first thought was of Daisy. She had come home from the hospital the night before with her arm in a cast. She was fine, but his father was quite upset. He had checked that branch and the rope a hundred times. And Daisy was tiny. He felt terribly guilty. He was trying to do something nice for his kids, and one of them ends up with a broken arm?

But Max knew it wasn't his father's fault. He knew exactly what had happened. The branch had been more than strong enough. He was told it was going to happen. But he certainly couldn't tell his father that.

Come and be with me...Bring your knife...

Max, without any hesitation, sat up in his bed and then got dressed. He went over to his desk and took his Boy Scout knife out of the drawer and slipped it into the front pocket of his jeans. He was only supposed to use it when he was with his father, but that thought did not even cross his mind. Within two minutes, he was walking out the front door.

On the ground at the base of the tree was the branch that had broken off with the rope and the tire still attached. Max cut the rope and sat down with his back against the warm bark of the trunk. He pulled the broken branch onto his lap and started whittling.

Unconsciously, he stripped the bark off of the branch. Faster and faster he ran the blade through the thick wood. Several times, he nicked his finger with the metal but did not react even once to the pain. Blood dripped from three or four different cuts on his fingers, but he didn't notice. The newly exposed wood became stained with his blood. It seemed to soak it up as if it were thirsty for it.

For hours, Max kept at his project. Blisters had formed on his palms, and the wood was actually hot from the knife blade running back and forth across the grain so quickly.

You are finished...Go now...

Max stood up and turned toward the trunk of the tree. He took his knife and carved three letters into the bark.

M....A....X

A few drops of blood from his thumb traveled down the blade and into one of the ruts of the letter X. The heartbeat became noticeably faster.

Thump thump...thump thump...thump thump...

Max took his finger and traced the other letters, giving each of them enough of his blood so they each had a reddish hue.

He put the knife back into his front pocket, picked up the spear he had just completed, and headed back towards the house.

THE ROWAN TREE
Chapter 18

Max was very proud of his woodwork. He had transformed the branch that had once held the tire swing into a long, smooth, and weighty spear. The shaft of it fit perfectly into his hand, and the point was sharp enough to hunt with.

Not that he was a hunter. He had never hurt an animal in his life. Maybe an ant or a bee that had been crawling on his arm, but that was about it. But there was nothing wrong with pretending he was a world-famous safari explorer.

Off to his right, Max saw a squirrel foraging in the grass. Quietly, he took a few steps closer. The squirrel froze, aware of the approaching threat. Max risked a few more steps to get as close as possible. The squirrel stood its ground. Max lifted his spear and, with all of his strength, sent the projectile flying towards the target.

The squirrel took off running the moment Max's arm moved forward. The spear landed with amazing accuracy in the exact spot where the animal had been. The point was buried eight inches into the ground. The balance of the weapon was perfectly crafted.

You need to practice...

Max decided he needed to give himself some target practice if he was going to be able to properly use his new weapon.

Go to the woodshed...Throw it at the door!

Max wandered back down towards the house, where he saw the woodshed. The door of the shed would make a perfect target. It had a square outline on the top of the frame, and if he missed, there was nothing nearby that could be damaged.

Max settled about twenty feet in front of the door and prepared to launch the spear at the target.

Wait....not yet....hold on....NOW!

Max hurled the spear. It flew straight and true directly at the square on the door. It crashed into the center and shattered the old wood, and half the length of the spear penetrated into the wooden shed.

"AHHHHHHH!" came a shriek from inside of the shed. "What the....HELP!" It was his father's voice, and he was panicked. He was inside the shed!

The fear in Max's stomach felt like a bolt of electricity. His legs became weak, like wet noodles.

"HELP ME!" his father yelled in pain.

The spear had traveled through the door where his father had been working and had stopped just after touching his head. He was pinned up against the wall with the weapon a centimeter away from entering his brain. Max raced to the door with the spear sticking out of it. The door was still closed. He didn't know what he would find inside. He yanked it open, and there stood his father, wide-eyed and breathing heavily, with a small puncture wound right in the middle of his forehead.

THE ROWAN TREE
Chapter 19
Darkness

One by one, each root was yanked from the ground, dirt falling to the side in clumps. And with each excruciatingly slow removal from the earth, the snakelike root was placed a few inches farther along the tree's intended path. The tips of the roots searched blindly for dirt, wiggling and twisting in the air until touching new soil and then burrowing once again deep into the ground. The roots alternated randomly like an octopus' tentacles searching and dragging the tree closer and closer towards the house.

A rabbit, eating grass under the cover of night, felt the ground shake and scurried down the nearest burrow. A root stabbed after it, twisted itself farther down into the ground, and then emerged with the rabbit caught in its tentacle.

Slowly, the appendage brought its struggling prey to the trunk and, with a sudden tightening, cracked the neck of the animal. The root then brought the meal closer and pushed it into the open knot at the center of the tree trunk. After depositing the rabbit, the root returned to the ground, where it continued to crawl across the dark field, closer to the house.

Closer to Max...

THE ROWAN TREE
Chapter 20
That Night

Max couldn't sleep a wink. He felt horrible. He had nearly killed his father, and that was just a day after his sister had broken her arm. Of course his parents were upset with him, and he felt ashamed. Why had he done something so stupid?

He could not sleep. His mind was racing, and his body seemed agitated all over. His skin itched, and he felt dirty, like he needed a shower. He kicked the covers off of him, hoping that the cooler air would be a relief. But after lying there for five minutes, he wasn't feeling any better.

The itching was even more pronounced on his chest. He was starting to feel like he was almost burning. He scratched with his fingernails, which seemed to be much longer than he was used to.

Finally, he couldn't take it any longer. He got out of his bed, put on his robe, and walked across the hall to the bathroom, scratching his chest with every step. He closed the door behind him and immediately turned the shower handle to get the warm water flowing.

As the bathroom began to fill with steam, he tried to relax and take deep breaths, inhaling the warm, humid air, trying to distract himself from the irritation. But his chest kept burning. He took off his robe and went and looked in the mirror.

There were scratch marks all over his torso from his fingernails trying to relieve the itching that had been driving him crazy. His chest was burning. It felt like he had been cut by a knife.

Max looked closer in the mirror through the steam. He took his hand and wiped an area of the mirror clean to get a better look. There was blood dripping down from what looked like fresh cuts on the right side of his chest. Then he realized that there was a fresh wound opening up on the left side.

As he stared, he could see his skin open up right in front of his eyes! The pain burned him, but it was muted by his confusion as to just what he was witnessing occur on his chest. The welts began rising and getting darker, and he could begin to see a pattern forming.

He could make out what looked like letters.
D....E....V....

The skin started opening next to the V and traveled down in a straight line. In a matter of seconds, the invisible blade made a sharp angle to the right, and Max saw the letter L clearly visible.

A minute later, the cutting had stopped, and Max stared in confusion at the word carved into his chest.

D...E...V...L...I...N

This meant nothing to him. He had no understanding of the meaning of this name. But the tree had marked him in the same way that Max had marked the tree—not as revenge or retribution, but as a connection between the two of them.

THE ROWAN TREE
Chapter 21
The Next Day

Daisy was out in the backyard. She was told not to go all the way to the tree by herself, but that seemed ridiculous now that she looked over at it. After all, the tree was only about twenty-five yards away from the house.

In fact, the tree was so close that she could see something glittering on one of the branches from where she was standing.

Attracted by the light coming from it, she wandered over in the direction of the tree to get a closer look. As she got within a few feet, she could see a gold medallion embedded in the trunk with part of a gold chain dangling from it.

She walked closer and tried to figure out what it was, but it was a too high. She put a foot on the trunk and reached up to grab the only branch that she could reach. As she touched the branch, she heard a rustling in the ground behind her and felt the tree sway a little bit. She let go and turned around to see what she expected to be a squirrel or something, but everything was still.

Daisy turned back to the branch and grabbed on with both hands. Struggling, she hoisted herself up and threw one leg over, straddling the huge limb. And then she heard the sound in the dirt once again. Out of the corner of her eye, she saw the root lift itself out of the ground and twist in the air. The tree also moved a bit, so she put one arm on the trunk to balance herself.

The gold medallion was only inches away, and she could reach up and touch part of the chain that hung down.

At that moment, Max turned the corner and saw Daisy precariously standing on the branch, reaching upward.

"Daisy! What are you doing? Get down from there!" Max screamed as he took off in a full sprint towards her.

"There's something really cool here in the tree!" she answered. "Come help me get it! It's gold, I think!"

Max ran, but before he could get there, the root that was already out of the ground curled up and twisted around Daisy's waist, yanking her from the limb. Another root disengaged itself from the earth and lashed out at Max, whipping him across the face to keep him from interfering.

STAY OUT OF THIS!

"LEAVE HER ALONE!" Max yelled with tears forming in his eyes.

The root holding Daisy curled around her more tightly and brought her closer to the trunk while Daisy screamed in fear.

"HELP ME, MAX! HELP ME!"

Max lunged forward once again, grabbing onto the root, trying to wrench it free from his baby sister. But it was no use. Max hung on to the root in midair, helpless to stop the twisting tentacle from delivering Daisy into the heart of the tree.

The knot in the trunk opened wider to allow Daisy's body to enter. Daisy struggled unsuccessfully, but the root had her arms and legs completely pinned to her body like a fly caught in a spider's web.

The tree began stuffing Daisy headfirst into its mouth. Max pulled against the root and braced both of his feet against the trunk, pushing with all of his strength to save his sister. It seemed to slow Daisy's descent into the bowels of the tree until another root twirled itself around Max's waist and flung him onto the ground.

Max watched in horror as he saw the soles of Daisy's shoes finally get swallowed. The trunk of the tree undulated, tying to swallow its meal like a snake trying to digest a large rodent.

"NOOOO!" he wailed. "Give her back! She's just a little girl!"

The medallion is for you, not her.

"What are you talking about?" Max said, answering the voice inside of his head.

A root stretched up to the top of the trunk, where the gold medallion lay encrusted into the bark of the tree. The tip burrowed its way under the rectangular medal and forced it free from its resting place. Delicately, the root twirled itself around the gold chain and held it before Max's face.

This is for you.

"I don't want it," Max said in an angry whisper. "I don't want anything from you. You took my sister!"

With that, the trunk began squeezing itself together, back and forth in rhythmic motions. A gurgling sound from deep within the knot, like a cat dealing with a hairball, began emanating from below.

Green fluid started oozing from the knot, spilling over the edge and running down the bark, pooling at Max's feet. Daisy's feet began to emerge. With each choking sound, a few more inches of her body were vomited from the tree.

Finally, Daisy fell to the ground, completely covered in the thin layer of greenish tree mucus. Max rushed to her, and just as he knelt by her side, she let out a sudden breath, expelling more of the wretched fluid from her lungs outward and onto Max's face. She sat up, gasping for breath and violently wiping the bile from her eyes and face.

Max lifted her and started to carry her away from the reach of the tree, but a root lashed out and held tightly to her ankle.

"LET HER GO!" Max demanded.

The root pulled harder, making it clear that she was not going anywhere. Slowly the other root holding the medallion dangled it once again in Max's face.

Put it on.

Max lowered Daisy to the ground. The root kept a tight hold of her ankle. He leaned his head forward, and the root draped the chain over his neck. The other root released Daisy's leg, and she scurried away backwards like a crab.

The roots buried themselves back into the ground while Max touched the medallion with his fingers.

Keep it on.

Max looked back at Daisy. He turned back to the tree.

"I will," he said, having no idea what he had done.

THE ROWAN TREE
Chapter 22

    They needed to explain what had happened to Daisy. Max's first instinct was to tell Daisy to keep it from their parents because he knew the tree would be angry. He had seen what it was capable of, and he knew his family was in danger. He would just keep his distance and never go near it again. But she was covered with a green, slimy substance. Even if she had been able to clean it off, her clothes were ruined. They had to say something.

    He convinced Daisy to just say that they were playing at the tree and she fell into the knot in the trunk. Daisy went along, but she was clearly scared out of her mind.

Later that night, Max jumped in the shower. He wasn't covered in the slime like his sister, but it was on his hands and arms from helping her.

He undressed but kept the medallion around his neck. He looked down at it. It lay across his chest, right in the center of the carving of the name DEVLIN, which was now a bright red, raised scar that was obviously permanent.

He examined it closer. It was a rectangular medallion with some sort of religious person on it. There was writing around the edges, but it was in a language that Max didn't recognize. He didn't want to wear it, but he was afraid of what might happen if he took it off.

He stepped under the hot water. It felt good to be under the stream and see the slime fall from his arms. The marks on his skin were even worse than the previous night. They didn't seem to itch anymore, but his skin now seemed very rough, like scales were forming where the deep scratches had been.

He rubbed the shampoo in his hair and realized that his hair was a mess. Leaves were everywhere. The more he scrubbed, the more leaves kept falling down into the bathtub and circled around the drain.

He looked down at the collection of leaves by his feet and noticed his toes. They looked different. Instead of five normal toes on each foot, they now looked deformed. His big toe was much longer, almost twice the size of a normal toe. And the two smallest toes had basically overlapped each other, as did the two middle toes. It looked like he now had just three on each foot. He looked like a reptile!

Max bent down to examine them, but he couldn't reach all the way. His skin was becoming so rough and thick that he couldn't bend his knees completely. His elbows wouldn't bend quite as far as they used to either.

He shut off the water. With great effort, he stepped out of the tub and onto the bath mat. He took the towel from the bathroom door and carefully dried his rough skin. He looked down at his deformed feet with horror.

He took the towel and wiped off the steam from the mirror to look at his face. There were leaves still in his hair. He leaned closer and reached up to grab one. But it didn't come out. It was attached to his head! He tried another, and then another. All of them were attached. They were growing out of him!

Max stepped back into the tub to try to rid himself of the leaves. He looked at his skin. It was so rough that it looked like pieces of wood. He looked back down to his feet. The toes were now completely intertwined. He stared at them, watching them move right in front of his eyes. The tips of what used to be his toes were blindly wiggling around, stretching to drink from the droplets of water coming from the shower.

Leaves were growing from his scalp, his skin was turning rough like bark, and his feet had morphed into roots! The shower was making it worse because the roots were able to get the water they needed to nourish the rest of him.   Max knew what was happening.

He was turning into a tree!

THE ROWAN TREE
Chapter 23

The water from the shower had sped up the process. Max's skin had been getting rough and coarse already, but once the roots that used to be his toes were able to drink, the rest of the body received the nourishment it needed to grow.

Painfully, Max stretched out his arm to shut of the shower. Because his skin was so rough, he could not completely bend his elbow. He turned his body sideways and leaned over, directing his arm, which was now more like a branch, towards the faucet. After several attempts, he was able to slow the water down to a trickle.

The roots struggled to find the remaining droplets of water. Max moved his legs backwards so that they couldn't reach the pool of water that was around the drain of the bathtub. As he moved backwards, the roots became frantic, pulling against his feet in a desperate attempt to drink.

Standing at the back of the bathtub, Max looked down at his deformed body. What was happening? His skin was much darker than before as a result of the bark forming over his entire body. The carving of DEVLIN across his chest was no longer as red. It now appeared more like an indentation, like a name written in cement that had dried. The gold medallion against his rough, dark skin now appeared brighter than ever.

That must be it! he thought. *The tree gave me the necklace. All of this started happening after it demanded that I put it on.*

Max knew immediately that the medallion had to be removed.

Don't touch it! We made a deal!

Max lifted his arms to his neck in an effort to grab the chain. His skin audibly cracked under the pressure of bending his elbows that far.

LEAVE IT ALONE!

He was able to force his elbow to bend enough to barely touch the chain at the top of his neck, but his fingers were becoming tiny twigs, and he could not control them enough to grasp the thin chain.

After struggling with it, he finally managed to put one of his clawlike hands through the chain holding the medallion. With all of his strength, he forced down with his bark-covered appendage and broke the chain, sending the medallion flying across the bathroom.

You lied. You broke your promise.

"Leave me alone!" he said out loud.

He crawled out of the tub, unable to bend his knee over the edge. After much effort, he got to his feet and wrapped himself in a towel. He did not want to be seen by his parents like this. He hoped that it would just go away. He knew the danger that the tree presented, and he didn't want his family getting involved.

After four or five tries, he was able to turn the doorknob and open the bathroom door. He shuffled as quickly as possible across the hall to his bedroom. Then he collapsed onto his bed. With great difficulty, he lifted his legs off the ground and curled up under the covers.

THE ROWAN TREE
Chapter 24

Max lay in his bed, certain that he was covered with leaves. He had never been so thirsty in all of his life. His newly forming body was craving water to nourish itself. But Max wanted the growth to stop, so he resisted the urge to drink.

Get Up...We need water...

Max tucked himself further under the blankets, trying to cover his ears from the voice coming from the tree. But it was of no use. The voice was emanating from inside his head. He had no ability to not hear it.

Come to me now...

Then he heard a different sound. This was a knocking sound. It was not the same communication he had been used to, in which he and the tree could have a silent conversation in their minds. This was a real sound.

It was a tapping on the window.

Tap...tap...tap................tap...tap...tap.

Can Max come out and play? It's Devlin...come outside.

Max did not want to look out of that window. He had a general understanding that somehow Devlin had something to do with the tree. He had felt at ease with the tree at first. But the tree had become progressively more menacing. The name Devlin now made him tremble. The tree was pure evil, and now it had a name.

Tap...tap...tap.

C'mon, Max...look outside...I have a surprise for you...

What could be at my window? Max thought. *I'm on the second floor.*

Max buried his head. "Go away," he said into his pillow.

Tap...tap...tap.

We had a deal. You knew better than to take it off. Now look out the window...

Max took the blanket off of his head. He sat up and looked nervously at the window, which was just a few feet from where he was sitting. With his limb, he pulled back the curtain just enough to get a peek outside. He expected to see the face of Devlin peering in with red, angry eyes and a huge drooling grin of fangs.

What he saw was a tree branch. The longest branch of the tree was tapping gently on his bedroom window, beckoning him to come out.

He leaned closer to the pane of glass and pulled back the curtain farther. The tree was right there. It was exactly next to the house and right outside his bedroom window...and it was twice the size of what it had been.

Max stared at the tree in the darkness. The tree was so close and the moon so bright that he could make out the subtle detail of each line in the bark. The dark, open knot in the trunk that had swallowed Daisy was just below the window, and he could see down into the depths of the trunk. He could read his name that he had carved into it.

But the most obvious and sinister thing about the tree was on the largest branch. The rope of the tire swing that had broken Daisy's arm was no longer lying on the ground under the tree. It now was a noose hanging on the edge of the limb. It hung ominously, waiting to be occupied.

Max stared at the thick brown rope, which had originally been hung as part of an innocent child's toy. It swung gently back and forth in an almost playful way.

Come out and play with me.

The end of the limb curled up like the fingers of a hand while the longest twig remained pointing at Max. In a slow, deliberate motion, it first turned and pointed at the noose. Then it turned back to Max and, with a curl of its knotty twig, beckoned him to come.

The black knot in the center of the trunk was now grotesquely agape in what seemed like a silent scream of agony. Except that it wasn't silent to Max. In his head, the scream of anguish was deafening.

The tree was demanding payback for the return of his sister.

THE ROWAN TREE
Chapter 25

Max closed the curtain and jumped back under the covers. As his head hit the pillow, the dried-out leaves on his head crackled and broke apart. He was so thirsty. But by refusing to drink, it seemed like the tree parts of him were not developing.

His legs were becoming restless. His feet, which had become more root than toes, were desperate to do their job, and they were beginning to move on their own in a search for any nearby water. Max pulled his knees up as far as his bark-covered skin would allow and kept the blankets wrapped around him as tightly as possible to keep his legs under his control.

TAP…TAP…TAP…TAP…TAP!

Come and join me now! Get out here where you belong!

The tapping was hard enough that it seemed like the window was about to break.

"STOP IT! LEAVE ME ALONE!" he screamed with tears in his eyes.

Walking by in the hallway, Max's father heard the commotion from the room. He opened the door and peeked his head in to check on him.

"Max?" he asked. "You okay in here? What's wrong?"

"Noth...nothing's wrong," stammered Max. "Just getting out of the shower...I'm fine," he said as he tucked the covers around him more tightly to hide his grotesque skin.

His father was still concerned.

"Well, it doesn't seem like you are okay," he said, walking over to the bed. "Why were you yelling a few seconds ago?"

And that's when he saw the top of Max's head.

"I thought you just got out of the shower?" he asked. "Why are there still a bunch of leaves in your hair?"

He reached down to pick them out. Max just turned to him and said, "Please help me, Dad."

He lifted one arm out from under the blankets and revealed the thing that used to be his arm but now was almost inhuman. His father's eyes opened wide.

He immediately pulled down the blanket to see his chest. He placed his palm on the rough skin and then looked back again at the claw that used to be his son's hand.

With both fear and concern, he threw the blanket off of him. He watched in horror as the roots that were once feet squirmed aimlessly like giant worms.

Suddenly, the window shattered as one of the roots from the rowan tree broke through the glass and grabbed Max by his ankle. Another one followed and grabbed his other leg. Max grabbed onto the corner post of the bed but couldn't get a firm grip because his hands didn't close properly.

Max's father lunged onto the pair of tentacles and tried to pry one of them off. It released Max's leg and attached itself to his father's wrist instead. A third root crawled through the window and grabbed his father by the waist and threw him across the room, slamming him into the far wall.

Like live electrical wires, the flailing roots returned to Max and dragged him out of his bed and onto the floor. Max's father got to his feet and sped across the room to grab hold of his son, but he was too late.

The tree picked up Max and pulled him through the shattered window.

THE ROWAN TREE
Chapter 26

Max's father ran to the window and watched as his son was carried through the air towards the tree. The tree pulled him into the canopy of leaves. And that's when he saw the noose at the end of the branch.

He ran out of Max's room and leaped down the stairs. In a second he had burst out of the front door and ran around the side of the house to where the tree now stood. He froze in disbelief as he watched several of the roots waving around wildly, trying to control Max, who was kicking and swinging his arms in a desperate attempt to escape.

The tree was trying to get Max's head in the noose, but the rope was swinging from the wild movements of the tree.

His father ran to the shed and frantically searched for a weapon he could use to save his son. In the corner, he saw his axe. He snatched it up and dashed back to the fight. The tree paid no attention to him. It was far too occupied with controlling its prey.

His father swung the axe as hard as he could and sent the steel blade driving through one of the roots at the exact point where it connected to the base of the tree. The tree released a squealing sound as it lost a part of its support system. Neon green sap burst out of the cut and sprayed over his father's face.

Another root lashed out and whipped Phil across his face, knocking the axe out of his hands and sending him barreling backwards. He scrambled to his feet and lunged for the axe just before the root was able to grab it.

With one motion, he picked the axe off the ground and swung it wildly in the direction of another root that was snaking its way towards him. The blade whirred through the air and caught the tip of the root, sending it flying off and releasing more green sap.

Max was still in the grips of the largest root, but for now, the tree was distracted with fending off the attack from his father. His father charged forward and this time sent the blade directly into the trunk of the tree.

The tree let out a high-pitched squeal, and more of the putrid sap spilled out onto the ground. Next, he lifted the axe over his head and came down on another root. But there were more roots coming out of the ground every second. Max's father just kept swinging the axe at each new root that slithered out of the ground.

In desperation, the tree gave up trying to put Max into the noose and just started squeezing him as hard as it could like a boa constrictor.

"DAD!" Max screamed. "I...I...I can't...breathe!"

His father looked up and saw the last large root that was trying to strangle his son. He ran at it, leaping in the air, swinging the axe in a wide circle. It connected and cut clean through. Max fell to the ground with the severed root still enveloping him like a cocoon. Sap poured out of the amputated stub of root, drenching Max. Still struggling for oxygen, his breathing was made even more difficult because of the fluid gushing onto his face.

His father turned around to look at the tree. He had chopped off six or seven roots already, but more were being yanked from the ground as he watched. The tree now had every root out of the ground. It stood facing Max and his father with the roots spread out to each side, ready to attack the way that a lizard makes itself bigger to scare its prey.

Max's father saw his opportunity and ran straight at the tree with his axe poised over his right shoulder. The roots all came down to attack their enemy at the same time, but not before he was able to land a strong blow into the trunk once again.

The roots grabbed him. His arms and legs were all controlled by the tree, and it started pulling him apart. But with no roots left in the earth, the final blow from the axe was enough to nudge the tree backwards. The tree, which now had nothing to balance it, began falling. It immediately let go of Max's father and frantically tried to replace its roots into the ground. But it was too late.

The tree began falling, teetering at first, then crashing to the ground with a tremendous thud. The roots, now all entirely out of the ground, flopped around like a school of fish gasping for air after being deposited on the deck of a boat.

The branches started moving, trying to push the tree back to a standing position. Max and his father stood back, praying that the tree would not be successful. They watched the two largest limbs dig themselves into the soil and lift the weight of the tree a few feet off of the ground. Slowly the trunk lifted.

But with a thundering *CRACK*, one of the limbs snapped in half, and the tree fell back down once again.

The ball of roots, losing energy, slowed their frantic attempts to grab hold of something and replant themselves.

Removed from its water source and drained of its green sap, the tree finally gave in. The tips of the roots started to curl into themselves. The only movements were the leaves blowing in the wind and the droplets of the green liquid periodically falling from the roots that had been damaged by the axe.

THE ROWAN TREE
Chapter 27

Finally safe, Max's father looked down at his son. He lay on the ground, barely able to keep his eyes open. He was trying to speak, but he was too exhausted and thirsty to make any understandable sounds.

He bent down to pick him up, feeling his skin, which now felt more like tree bark than anything human. Max winced in pain as his father lifted him from the ground, bending his body and causing some of the bark to crack.

But although he was able to lift Max's torso off the ground, his feet were stuck. His feet, which were now roots, had found their way to the soil and were searching desperately to find him water. His father set him back down and clawed at the ground, trying to unearth his son's feet from the soil.

A few seconds later, he was able to yank on Max's ankles and free him from the earth. Max's feet sought the dirt again, but he was able to pick Max up fast enough to prevent them from reattaching.

"Thirsty," Max whispered.

Max's father knew what he had to do. First, he had to get Max safely inside and give him water so his body would not wither away. And secondly, he had to get to the woodshed, find the gas can, and make sure the tree was gone forever.

EPILOGUE

THE ROWAN TREE
Chapter 28
Two Years Later

The hair was really not a problem. The easy
solution, of course, was simply to keep it short in a crew
cut. And with heavy applications of moisturizer every
day, Max was able to retain some flexibility in his skin.
His upper body now appeared just to have a fairly
serious case of psoriasis.

A prosthetic company was able to come up with
an amazing device that allowed limited maneuverability
of his hands so he was able to operate a computer and
cell phone. He even had a game system with a special
controller that he could operate with voice commands.

Max was adapting bravely to his handicap.

But his legs presented a challenge that the doctors could not overcome.

The good news is that he didn't have to be planted outside. Given his smaller size, he was able to stay indoors. As long as he stayed by the window during the day, he was able to get the sunlight he needed to survive.

His pot stayed in the corner of the kitchen during the days so that he could get the greatest amount of sunshine. That's where he and his mother would work on homeschooling. And in the evenings, his father would move the pot into the living room so that Max and the family could watch television together.